YIKES, Santa-CLAWS!

Pamela Butchart
& Sam Lloyd

BLOOMSBURY

LONDON   NEW DELHI   NEW YORK   SYDNEY

It was late on Christmas Eve,
when Mummy gently said,
"Santa Claus will soon be here
so snuggle up in bed."

But where were the jolly jingle bells?
The hearty **HO! HO! HO!**?
And who was this green scaly creature
stomping through the snow?

YIKES, Santa-CLAWS!

He slipped right
down the chimney.

and landed
with a SMACK!

"Oh, toe-bells," cried **Santa-CLAWS,**
"I've squashed EVERYTHING in my sack!"

The dino-tots crept down the stairs
and – oh! – what did they see?
A crunching, munching, scaly beast
EATING the Christmas tree!

He tried on Dad's
new reindeer pants,

and Mum's red sparkly shoes!

He pulled the
Christmas crackers,

scoffed the
turkey in one bite.

BURP!

He burped out carols loudly
and gave the cat a fright!

Then **Santa-CLAWS** stomped outside,
leaving a trail of stinky poos.
The dino-tots raced upstairs
to tell their mum the news!

He guzzled his way
from house to house,

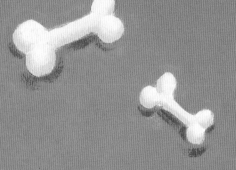

till there was nothing
left to eat.

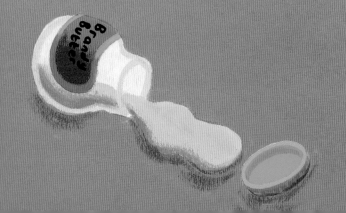

But then - quite fortunately -
he saw a starry treat.

YIKES, Santa-CLAWS!

The tree began to wobble,
then fell down with a crash.

"Someone stop him," the dinos roared,
"or Christmas will be trashed!"

But, suddenly, a

HO! HO! HO!

echoed loud and clear.

Look! The real
Santa CLAUS - hooray!
And everyone gave a cheer.

"What a naughty dino!"
Santa Claus exclaimed . . .

"I'll put it right," sobbed Santa-CLAWS.
"I really feel ashamed."

He cleared up all the poo and drool,

and mended the broken toys.

Then helped to deliver presents
to the dino girls and boys.

"That's better," boomed out Santa.
"Now let's get home for tea."
And next Christmas do remember . . .
leave the job to me!

YIKES, Santa-CLAWS!

For Laurasaurus - my new little sister!
With thanks to Alison, Emma and Becky ~ PB

For my little sunbeam, with love from Mummy ~ SL

Bloomsbury Publishing, London, New Delhi, New York and Sydney

First published in Great Britain in 2014 by Bloomsbury Publishing Plc
50 Bedford Square, London, WC1B 3DP

Text copyright © Pamela Butchart 2014
Illustrations copyright © Sam Lloyd 2014
The moral rights of the author and illustrator have been asserted

A CIP catalogue record for this book is available from the British Library

ISBN 978 1 4088 5137 1 (HB)
ISBN 978 1 4088 5138 8 (PB)
ISBN 978 1 4088 5136 4 (eBook)

Printed in China by Leo Paper Products, Heshan, Guangdong

1 3 5 7 9 10 8 6 4 2

www.bloomsbury.com

BLOOMSBURY is a registered trademark of Bloomsbury Publishing Plc

All papers used by Bloomsbury Publishing are natural, recyclable products
made from wood grown in well-managed forests.
The manufacturing processes conform to the environmental regulations of the country of origin